HAND-ME-DOWN MAGIC

MAGIC

CRYSTAL BALL FORTUNES

ALSO BY COREY ANN HAYDU

Hand-Me-Down Magic #1:
Stoop Sale Treasure

COREY ANN HAYDU

HAND-ME-DOWN
MAGIC

CRYSTAL BALL FORTUNES

illustrated by
LUiSA URiBE

KATHERINE TEGEN BOOKS
An Imprint of HarperCollins Publishers

Katherine Tegen Books is an imprint of HarperCollins Publishers.

Hand-Me-Down Magic #2: Crystal Ball Fortunes
Text copyright © 2020 by Corey Ann Haydu
Illustrations copyright © 2020 by Luisa Uribe

ISBN 978-0-06-287827-4 — ISBN 978-0-06-297826-4 (pbk)

Typography by David DeWitt
20 21 22 23 24   PC/LSCH   10 9 8 7 6 5 4 3 2 1
❖
First Edition

For my daring and delightful nieces and
nephews, the best cousins my kid could hope
for: Ellen, Amy, Shane, Brennan and Milena
– C.A.H.

For my mom
– L.U.

ALMA'S HOME
THAT FINALLY REALLY
FEELS LIKE HOME →

TITI ROSA, EVIE,
AND A LOT OF
LAUGHTER LIVE HERE →

DEL'S HOME WITH
HER FAMILY AND THE
PERFECT PLACE TO
HIDE SOMETIMES →

THIS IS WHERE
YOU CAN FIND
LOVE, CREMITA,
AND ABUELITA →

THE CURIOUS
COUSINS
SECONDHAND
SHOPPE →

86 ½
TWENTY-THIRD AVENUE

ABUELITA'S
WILD AND MARVELOUS
BACKYARD GARDEN

1

Delightful and Daring

-Del-

There were only sixteen hours to go before Del's Delightful and Daring Dress-Up Party. She had been counting down the hours for an entire week. It was a tradition because Del loved birthdays, and Abuelita loved hosting parties, and the whole family loved cake and party hats and singing one round of "Happy Birthday" followed by one round of "Feliz Cumpleaños" at the top of their lungs.

"How many people are coming?" Alma asked.

She was putting together goody bags for the guests. She'd helped Del pick out stickers and sparkly pens and three different kinds of chocolate. "This seems like a lot of chocolate." She gestured to the enormous pile. Their littlest cousin, Evie, couldn't stop eyeing it. It was so tall that Alma couldn't see over the top of it from her seat at Abuelita's kitchen counter. The pile was so tall that Evie had named it Chocolate Mountain and said they should keep it just like that forever.

"Like a million people," Del said. "Pretty much everyone ever. And they're all going to be dressed up! I can't wait to see what everyone's wearing!"

"A million?" Evie repeated. She was bouncing up and down on her toes. "Really?"

"No, not really," Del said. She rolled her eyes at Alma. But Alma looked nervous, like she thought there really might be a million people shoved into Abuelita's apartment tomorrow too. "More like twenty. But still. That's a lot. That's more than were at my party last year. But I'm going to be another year older, so it makes sense."

"Twenty is a lot less than a million," Evie said, huffing. "You're not very good at math, Del."

"Not as good as you, I guess," Del said, laughing.

Evie thought about this. "Do you think I'm good enough at math to count all these chocolate bars?" she asked.

"Why don't you try?" Del said. Evie started counting pieces of chocolate very loudly. So loudly, in fact, that Abuelita and Titi Rosa came into the kitchen to see what all the fuss was about.

Abuelita made a startled noise—"Oh!"—and smiled. Del and Alma turned to see what she was looking at. She was facing the window that looked out at the backyard. And right there, perched on the birdbath, was a little black kitten. It was dipping its paws into the birdbath, then shaking them off, over and over, like it was trying to figure out something very important.

"What a darling gatito!" Abuelita said. "¡Hola, mi gato!" she called out to the kitten.

The kitten jumped in surprise, and the jump made it stumble all the way into the birdbath with a cute kitteny splash. Del thought the kitten might be scared, taking that fall. But instead it seemed interested in the water. It licked it. It pawed at it. It jumped out of it, then right back in.

Del had seen a lot of stray cats before, but never one that acted anything like this one.

"It's time to start winding down," Titi Rosa said, directing them away from the window and the now-very-wet kitten.

"But we have so much decorating left to do!" Del said.

"And so much chocolate to eat—I mean count!" Evie said.

"I've never been to a delightfully daring dress-up party," Alma whispered to Del. She sounded nervous.

"Don't be a fraidycat!" Del said. "This party is going to be perfect."

"I hope so," Alma said. "And I'm not a fraidy-cat. I just get scared of new things sometimes."

"How can you be scared when you're going to be wearing this?" Del ran to the closet where she'd been storing her big surprise: two big, fluffy boas. They'd been planning their costumes for the party for a while, but this would be the perfect addition, Del was sure. She wrapped the orange boa around Alma and the purple one around herself.

"What can go wrong when you have a boa?" Del asked. She twirled her purple boa and did a little birthday dance.

Alma put her boa around Del's shoulders.

"You're the birthday girl," she said. "You should have both."

"Are you sure?" Del asked. She liked wearing both boas. It made her extra glamorous.

"Positive," Alma said.

Del grinned. "Tomorrow will be the best day ever."

2

A Possibly Perfect Present

-Alma-

Alma, Del, and Evie stood in front of Titi Rosa's full-length mirror admiring their costumes. Alma knew Evie loved Titi Rosa's mirror. It was carved with birds and flowers. Plus, it was fun to dance in front of.

Alma usually liked the mirror too. But today she didn't think she looked quite right in it. She was wearing an old dress of Abuelita's from when she was a little girl. It was blue and puffy and shiny. She was also wearing a pair of butterfly wings that Del said looked perfect with the dress.

"Are you sure this looks okay?" Alma asked her cousin.

"Definitely," Del said. "Do you think I need another tutu?" Del was already wearing three tutus, a flower crown, and sparkly leggings.

"Yes!" Evie said. "You definitely need more tutus." Evie had on a Superman T-shirt, a pair of overalls, and the big straw hat that Abuelita used when she gardened. She had a sticker of a star on her left cheek.

"I think three's the right amount," Alma said.

"I wish I had a purple tutu to match my purple boa," Del said.

Alma's heart sank. She wished she'd known that Del wanted a purple tutu. That would have been the perfect gift for her birthday! Alma had spent the whole week trying to think of what Del would want. She'd gone to every store in the neighborhood, trying to imagine what Del might like best. She'd considered polka-dotted leggings from Dotty Designs, strawberry jam from the farmer's market, and a comic about a crime-fighting unicorn from the comic-book store. None of those things was quite right.

Finally, Alma had gone back to Curious Cousins Secondhand Shoppe. Just as she'd hoped, Abuelita had led her to the back room, where they stored all kinds of donations and odds and ends that they hadn't put out in the store yet. Alma had found something for Del. She hoped it was perfect. She thought it might be perfect. It needed to be perfect.

"I think you look great," Alma said. "Very birthday-ish."

"Do I look delightfully daring?" Del asked.

"You do," Alma said. She really meant it, too.

Downstairs in Abuelita's living room, Del's parents were decorating her birthday cake, and Alma's parents were hard at work blowing up balloons in every possible color. Abuelita and Titi Rosa were setting up games to play. Titi Clara and Uncle Andy were trying to decide what music everyone would want to dance to.

"How should I help?" Alma asked.

"You can answer the door," Abuelita said. "Let in our guests."

"All of them? By myself?" Alma asked. Her hands felt a little sweaty. Her heart felt sort of fast.

"I'll help!" Evie said. Alma had never been so happy to have Evie butting in.

"Before the guests come, we have a present to give you, Del," Titi Rosa said.

"But it's not present time yet," Del said. Still, she held out her hands, ready to open up her very first delightful and daring present.

"It's not the kind of present you open," Abuelita said.

"Oh," Del said. "Well, where is it?"

"It's right here." Abuelita smiled. Her eyebrows

wiggled. Her wiggling eyebrows seemed to make her ears wiggle too. Alma tried to make her eyebrows and ears wiggle, but it wasn't very easy.

"I don't see anything," Del said, spinning around and around.

"Your present," Abuelita said, "is that you, Alma, and Evie can sleep outside tonight. Here in the garden. In your very own tent."

Del screeched. "That's the best present ever! Thank you, thank you, thank you!"

"De nada, mi cielo," Abuelita said. She was smiling almost as big as Del.

Del jumped up and down. She twirled around and around. The doorbell rang, and Del screeched with happiness again.

But Alma froze. She was feeling so nervous about all the new people at the party. Evie grabbed her hand and pulled her to the door. Alma knew it was just because Evie wanted to get her there faster, but she was happy to be holding her cousin's hand anyway. The doorbell rang again. The party was really, finally beginning.

3

Madame Del

-Del-

Before she knew it, Del's party was filled with friends and family, all dressed up. 86 ½ Twenty-Third Avenue was dressed up too. There were silver streamers everywhere, and balloons in every color of the rainbow.

Del's neighbor Anna had on a sundress, four different silk scarves, and a cowboy hat. Her friend Cassie showed up in a sparkly dance costume and a vampire cape. Even Oscar, the best dog in the whole neighborhood, came by with his owners, Cora and Javi. Cora and Javi apologized for not having on anything delightful or daring, but Del forgave them because

they'd dressed Oscar up in a formal tux. He
had a little bow tie and a little jacket and even a
little top hat strapped to his head. Del thought

he looked very dignified.

Felix Sanderson was the last to arrive, and Del thought he looked best of all. He was wearing a brown vest with fringe all over it and plaid pants and a shirt that must have been from Dotty Designs and a hat he'd decorated himself with pictures of Del's face and the words *HAPPY BIRTHDAY DEL* in green puffy paint.

"Wow," Del said.

"I like birthdays," Felix said. He handed over something else he'd made. It was a poster of Del's face. And a paper bag filled with pictures of birthday hats and birthday cakes and birthday presents. "Pin the Birthday on the Del," Felix said.

Del was delighted. She loved games of all kinds, but especially, it turned out, games about her.

"Can we play right now?" Del asked.

Everyone played three rounds of Pin the Birthday on the Del, and Evie won every time.

They had a costume contest and awarded Felix the top prize for his Del-themed outfit.

They ate pizza with pepperoni and pizza with four different cheeses and two different onions and pizza with jalapeño and pizza with bacon and Felix's favorite, pizza with french fries on top. They ate chocolate-caramel cupcakes and red velvet cupcakes and pumpkin cupcakes and plain old vanilla cupcakes with vanilla icing.

Eventually, Evie led everyone outside to Abuelita's garden for a game of kick the can.

"I don't know the rules," Alma said.

"That's okay!" Del said.

"I'd rather watch," Alma said.

"Just try," Del said. And Alma did, but her knees shook the whole time. Still, Del was impressed that she tried.

Evie won kick the can, even though she was the youngest and the smallest.

Finally, it was time for presents. Del opened up boxes of board games and art supplies and headbands. She unwrapped a soccer ball and a penguin night-light and four new books.

She was saving Alma's present for last.

Alma brought it over, looking more nervous than ever. "I hope you like it," Alma said.

"I will," Del said.

"But I hope you *really* like it," Alma said.

"If you don't like it, I'll take it!" Evie offered, and everyone laughed.

Alma's present for Del was wrapped in gold paper and a silver ribbon. She'd tied a daisy on top, and somehow, like magic, it wasn't drooping yet.

Del admired the wrapping for a second before tearing it to pieces. What was inside was even better.

"Oh," Del said.

"Ohhhh," Evie said.

"Ohhhhhhhhhh," the rest of the guests said.

Even though no one had ever seen one in real life before, they all knew exactly what it was.

A crystal ball. The kind that could tell people's fortunes. It was even better than ones Del had seen on TV and in movies. This crystal ball looked ancient, and Del was sure it had been passed down through a hundred magical generations, just like all the best magic. It was a hard-to-describe color: sort of purple and sort of silver and sort of yellow and sort of clear. It reminded Del a little of the mood rings she and

Alma had found at one particularly great stoop sale. The crystal ball stood on a golden stand that needed a good shining. The stand had carvings of birds and flowers etched onto its surface, just like Titi Rosa's beautiful mirror. It looked nearly as magical as the crystal ball itself!

Del leaped up and hugged Alma so tight that Alma gasped.

"Can you believe it?" Del said to her parents and Abuelita, who were watching all the fun.

"Pretty!" her mother said.

"Fancy!" her father said.

"Be careful," Abuelita said.

The crystal ball was better than anything Del could have wished for. She had always wanted to be able to tell fortunes. She wanted to predict the future.

She couldn't wait.

And she wouldn't wait.

She sat cross-legged on the ground and put her new crystal ball in front of her. She closed her eyes to concentrate. She adjusted her three tutus and made sure her flower crown was on tight.

Fortune-telling was serious business.

"I am Madame Del, the magical fortune-teller of 86 ½ Twenty-Third Avenue! I am here to tell your fortune!"

4

Fortunes for Everyone

-Alma-

Madame Del turned out to be a very good fortune-teller. Alma had known she would be.

When Cassie stepped up to have her fortune told, Madame Del closed her eyes and made a humming noise. When she opened her eyes, she put her face very close to the crystal ball.

"Oh!" Madame Del said. "I see . . . I see a woman in red!"

"A woman in red?" Cassie asked. "Like, a scary woman in red?"

Madame Del brought her nose all the way to the surface of the crystal ball. "No," Madame Del said. "She looks very nice."

Alma was relieved. She didn't want a scary woman in red showing up. She didn't want anyone at all to get a bad fortune, even if she wasn't sure the crystal ball was real.

A few minutes later, Cassie's mother came to pick her up. She was wearing a red dress!

"Wow," Cassie said. "That's amazing!"

"Did you see what Cassie's mom was wearing when she dropped her here?" Alma asked Del.

"Of course not!" Madame Del said. "Who's next?"

"Me!" Felix Sanderson said. He stepped up to the crystal ball. He straightened his bow tie.

Madame Del closed her eyes. She made a humming noise. She rubbed the crystal ball. Alma wondered how she knew to do all that. If someone gave Alma a crystal ball, she'd have no idea how to use it.

"I see cake," Madame Del said.

"I just had cake," Felix said.

Madame Del leaned in closer to the ball. "Well, I see more cake," she said.

Felix shrugged and stood up. He stood up right on top of a discarded cupcake someone had left on the ground! His shoes were covered in cake!

"Right again!" Felix said.

Madame Del grinned.

Alma couldn't believe it. The crystal ball was really working!

"Your turn, Alma!" Madame Del said. But Alma was scared. And shy. She didn't want everyone watching her while her fortune got told.

"Not right now," Alma said.

"Don't be a fraidycat!" Madame Del said. Alma blushed. She didn't like being called a fraidycat.

Luckily, Evie interrupted. She sat down right in front of the crystal ball. "Tell my fortune!" she demanded.

Madame Del closed her eyes. She took a deep breath. She put her hands just above the crystal ball. When she opened her eyes, she leaned in close.

"Aha!" Madame Del said. "I see water!"

"Are we going to the beach?" Evie said. Alma laughed. Evie loved the beach. She asked if they were going to the beach every single morning.

"I don't know," Madame Del said. "I just see water."

"I bet it's the beach!" Evie said. "Let me go get my swimsuit! Oh, and my bucket and shovel! Where did we put the umbrella?" Evie was off and running. But before she was able to get any of her beach things, Titi Rosa scooped her up.

"Bathtime!" Titi Rosa said.

"Noooooo!" Evie cried.

"I was right again!" Madame Del said.

Maybe it really does work, Alma thought. Madame Del looked very proud, and Alma was proud too. She had gotten Del the perfect present. And not only that, but it might be really and truly magical!

Del told fortunes until it was time for her guests to return home. Alma thought that meant it was time to put the crystal ball away, but she always underestimated her cousin.

"Your turn, Alma," Del said with a big birthday-girl grin. And because Del was the birthday girl, Alma couldn't possibly refuse.

5

Madame Alma

-Del-

"How do you do it?" Alma asked. She might have been scared, but she was curious too. And if Del knew anything, it was that a curious cousin was an excellent thing.

"I just look at it, close my eyes, and when I open them again, there's an image in the ball!" Del said. She couldn't stop rubbing her new crystal ball. It was the best present she'd ever gotten. She wished she knew how to thank Alma for it.

"That doesn't sound so scary," Alma said.

"It's not scary at all!" Del said.

"It really works?" Alma said.

"You saw it work!" Del said. Sometimes Del and Alma disagreed about things like magic, but today Alma wouldn't be able to argue with Madame Del. She had told so many fortunes perfectly!

Alma stepped closer to the ball. Then closer again. Still, she was frowning. Del didn't want her to be frowning or scared or shy or nervous. Finally, she thought of one thing that might help.

"How about you tell *my* fortune?" Del said. "I hereby declare you Madame Alma."

Alma grinned. "Madame Alma? Really?" she said.

"Absolutely!" Del said. She curtseyed to Madame Alma, and Madame Alma curtseyed back. Suddenly, Alma wasn't scared Alma anymore. She was Madame Alma, magnificent fortune-teller. And Del would find her some customers. All their guests might have left, but

86 ½ Twenty-Third Avenue was always filled with family.

"I need some practice before I tell a birthday fortune," Madame Alma said.

"Good idea," Del said. She wanted the best birthday fortune she could get, after all. "Wait right here."

Del ran through the building. She found Abuelita in her kitchen and her father on their fire escape where he liked to read sometimes. Finally, Del found Titi Clara on the stoop, about to walk to her own building a few doors down. "You have to come with me," she told each of them. "It's very important." She led them all to Abuelita's living room, where the crystal ball and Madame Alma were both sitting on the floor.

"Abuelita, Madame Alma would like to tell your fortune," Del said. Abuelita gave a serious nod and sat down across from Madame Alma. Del handed over the crystal ball. She put Madame Alma's hands on its cool surface. "Close your eyes," she said, and Madame Alma did. "Open them again," Del said.

"I have to make my magical noise first," Madame Alma said.

Del beamed. Finally, her cousin understood magic!

Madame Alma took a big breath and blew it out in a long, magical sigh. Then she made a humming noise. Then whistled three little notes and waved her fingers around. Del was impressed.

At last, Madame Alma opened her eyes. She looked long and hard at the crystal ball. She tilted her head one way, and then the other. She stood up, so that she could see the top of the crystal ball. She lifted the ball up so she could look at the bottom.

"I see a crystal ball," Madame Alma said.

"But what do you see inside?" Del asked.

Madame Alma shook the ball. She turned it over and over in her hands. She held it up to the light.

"Aha!" Madame Alma said. "I see it!"

Del knew her cousin had some magic inside her. They were cousins, after all! And magic ran in their family. She couldn't wait to hear what magical fortunes Madame Alma would reveal.

6

Something Black and Fuzzy

-Alma-

Madame Alma had hoped the fortunes would be very clear, but it wasn't exactly the way Del had described. She didn't see much in the crystal ball. Mostly just colors and almost-shapes. She guessed it was her job to figure out what those fortunes were supposed to be.

She looked at Abuelita's hopeful face, then back at her crystal ball. She saw some yellow light. Kind of like the moon. "I see the moon," Madame Alma declared. "A very beautiful moon."

"¡Que lindo!" Abuelita said. Alma knew Abuelita loved the moon. Sometimes she painted pictures of it, and sometimes she sat under it at night, and sometimes she told the family stories about all the magical things the moon could do. "An evening in the moonlight. I can't wait."

"Who's next?" Madame Alma asked.

"I'll go," Tío Victor said. Del's father was always brave.

Madame Alma closed her eyes and hummed and wiggled her fingers. She looked deep into the crystal ball. She saw something blue and shiny. She tried to think about what the shape might be. It was sort of rectangular, she thought. Maybe a car? "I see a blue car!" she declared.

"A new one?" Tío Victor asked. He was smiling. Del's family car was white and very old. He was always complaining about it.

"Yes," Madame Alma said. "A new blue car."

"Well, that's great news!" he said. Madame Alma was liking this more and more! She had delivered two wonderful fortunes. She couldn't wait for them to come true.

When Titi Clara sat in front of her, Madame Alma was pretty sure she saw red. "A dozen red roses!" she said. Titi Clara looked very pleased with this. "I've never gotten flowers from someone before," she said. "And I do love roses!"

For Evie's fortune, Madame Alma looked long and hard. She didn't see any colors or shapes. Just her own face reflected back at her. "A . . . mirror?" Madame Alma said.

"Titi Rosa's mirror?" Evie asked. She put her hand over her heart.

"I think so. Yes," Alma said.

"Titi Rosa is going to give me her amazing mirror!" Evie squealed with delight.

Finally, it was Del's turn to have her fortune told.

Madame Alma hesitated for a moment. It was a very big responsibility to tell the birthday girl's fortune, and she didn't want to mess it up. Plus, she wasn't sure exactly what she was seeing in there. Sometimes it seemed like she wasn't seeing much at all.

Still, Madame Alma leaned over the crystal ball. She closed her eyes as tight as she could. She hummed very loudly. She whistled and wiggled her fingers and, she was pretty sure, finally managed to wiggle her eyebrows and ears too. She opened her eyes and lifted the crystal ball up in the air. She put it down, very gently. She waved her hands above it and picked it up one more time.

"I see . . . ," she said. But she didn't see anything. "I see . . ." But still, there was nothing in there. Not even a speck of light or a hint of a shape. "I see . . . black?"

"Black?" Del asked.

Madame Alma tried again. It wasn't just black, she thought. It was sort of blurry. Or fuzzy? Yes. Black and fuzzy. "I see something black and fuzzy," Madame Alma said.

"Black and fuzzy," Del repeated.

"Maybe . . . a dog? Or . . . I don't know . . . a cat?"

"A *cat*?" Del asked. "You see a black cat?"

"Yes," Madame Alma said. She wanted to sound sure. She wanted to be a good fortune-teller for her cousin.

Del's face got very serious. And very pale.

"You love animals," Alma said.

"A black cat is bad luck," Del said. "The worst kind of luck. Everyone knows that. It's why they're around at Halloween. Because they're scary. And I know it's true because last year Cassie saw a black cat, and that same day she broke

her leg playing soccer even though she was the best soccer player in school."

"Oh!" Alma said. "Oh no! I must have been wrong. It's probably a black dog. Or a black raccoon. Or, I don't know, a black boa?"

"No," Del said. "You said a black cat. A very unlucky black cat on my birthday."

"I'm sorry!" Alma said. "I'm sure I'm wrong! None of my fortunes have come true yet. Yours all came true right away. I'm not good at this the way you are."

Del looked a little less nervous. "That's true," she said.

"You have nothing to be afraid of," Alma said.

Del nodded. She didn't look sure, though. She looked scared. And Alma wasn't used to Del being the scared one. She didn't like it. She didn't like it one bit.

A Full Moon

-Del-

Del wasn't in the mood for a backyard slumber party anymore.

"We saw a black kitten out there yesterday," she said. "I need to stay away from all black cats."

"You're afraid of that kitten?" Alma asked. She'd never heard of Del being afraid of anything at all.

"I'm not *afraid*," Del said. "I'm just being careful because of my fortune. I can't let a black cat cross my path. I need to just sleep in my own bed. And stay inside tomorrow. And the next day. And probably forever."

"You were so excited about your backyard slumber party," Alma said. "Let's at least give it a try."

Del wanted to say no, but Alma was giving her big worried eyes, and Evie was pulling on her arm, and Del *had* always wanted to have a sleepover in the backyard. This might be her only chance. And besides, Alma was right. None of Madame Alma's fortunes had come true the way Del's had. Maybe it would be okay.

Alma, Del, and Evie walked out to the backyard. Alma had secretly set up the tents while Del was saying goodbye to all her guests. One tent was for Abuelita, and the other was for the cousins. In the cousin tent, Alma had laid out three sleeping bags and three pillows and all the cozy blankets she could find at 86 ½ Twenty-Third Avenue. And best of all, Alma had decorated the tent with streamers and balloons and a big shiny

banner that said *Happy Birthday!* on it.

"Oh, wow," Del said. "This is so cool. How did you do this? It's . . ."

"Magical!" Alma finished Del's sentence with Del's favorite word. But Del wasn't so sure she wanted to hear that word right now.

"And I brought out cupcakes!" Evie announced way too loudly. Abuelita had already said no when they asked if they could eat cupcakes out in the tent before bed.

"Shhhhh," Del and Alma said together. But Evie couldn't keep a secret.

"Look!" Evie said. She had one of Abuelita's cozy blankets around her shoulders. She opened up the blanket to show the box of leftover cupcakes she'd been hiding underneath.

Del smiled. Maybe everything really would be fine! Maybe there was no such thing as a bad fortune! Maybe Madame Alma hadn't seen a black cat after all! Their tent was so pretty. Those cupcakes looked even better now than they had at the party. Alma had brought out her mother's phone and was playing music to dance to. It was everything a slumber party was supposed to be.

But before Del could take even one bite of cupcake, they heard a sound.

"Oh no!" Abuelita cried.

Del, Alma, and Evie ran out of their tent. "What's wrong?" Del asked when they got to Abuelita's tent. Everything seemed normal. There was a sleeping bag and a pillow and her own stash of cupcakes, in spite of her rules.

"What is it?" Alma asked.

Abuelita pointed up. All three girls tilted their heads to follow her finger. She was pointing

at a big, gaping hole in the tent. A hole so big that when you looked up, you could see the full moon in the sky.

"Well, that's sort of pretty," Alma said.

"Can we stay in *this* tent instead?" Evie asked. "This is so cool!"

"The moon," Del said, her voice a little shaky. "Just like your fortune said." Del had been hoping maybe Madame Alma wasn't so good at telling fortunes. But here was Abuelita underneath the moon, just like Madame Alma had predicted.

And then it started to rain. Within moments, everything in the tent was soaking wet.

"Oh no!" Abuelita said. "This isn't what I expected when you told my fortune!"

Del looked at Alma. "This isn't a very good fortune at all," she said.

Before she finished her sentence, Del heard a little purring sound. A cat. Maybe a kitten. Maybe a little black kitten. She ran straight inside the house and all the way upstairs, and refused to come back downstairs no matter how many cupcakes Evie offered her or how many times Alma said the fortune was probably wrong.

Del was pretty sure she wouldn't be leaving the house ever again.

8

Look Out Below

-Alma-

In the morning, Alma found Del and Tío Victor on the front stoop. Del and her dad liked to sit out there in the mornings. This morning, they looked like they were watching something. Tío Victor's white car was parked right in front of the building, but they weren't watching that. A few women on the corner were in an argument about where to get coffee, but Alma didn't think they were watching that. Next door, a painter was painting the shutters on their neighbor's building. But that's not what they were watching either.

Del and Tío Victor were watching something across the street, in the playground. Alma squinted. It was Evie, chasing squirrels and

laughing. Del was pretty sure she could hear her chattering away at them, too, telling them all her secrets. Evie could find the fun in absolutely anything.

Del and her father were both holding forks.

The leftover cupcakes were sitting between them.

"Cake for breakfast?" Alma said. She'd never had anything but breakfast food for breakfast. Her mother sometimes made breakfast for dinner, though, and she loved that. Maybe she would love this, too?

"We always do it the day after birthdays," Del said.

"Take a fork," Tío Victor said. "Taste a few."

Alma happily did. It turned out all flavors of cupcake tasted even better in the morning.

"Do you feel better today?" Alma asked Del.

"She's on the lookout for cats," Tío Victor said. "I promised her there wouldn't be any out on a busy street in the morning." That seemed true to Alma.

"Abuelita's fortune came true last night, so mine probably will too," Del said.

"That was just a coincidence," Alma said. She was pretty sure this was right. After all, she hadn't predicted a rainstorm, just the moon.

"You really think so?" Del asked. She took an extra-big bite of cupcake. Del wouldn't admit to being scared, but Alma had never seen Del so frightened. In fact, she'd never really seen her scared at all. But if Del was the scared one, that meant Alma would have to be the brave one. She took a deep breath.

"I really think so," Alma said. "We should do something fun today. To make up for last night. We could even invite a bunch of people over again. Or do something silly. Wear our costumes to the store. Or sing a song in the middle of the street. Or tell fortunes with the crystal ball for everyone at the playground." Alma looked at Del. She wanted Del to look brave and happy and unscared again. She thought maybe the corners of Del's mouth were turning up. She thought maybe her eyes were starting to sparkle with excitement. She thought maybe Del wasn't looking for a black cat anymore.

"That does sound fun . . . ," Del said.

But before Del could agree to a plan for the day, they heard the painter next door shout "Watch out below!" He had dropped his can of paint. Alma, Del, and Tío Victor ran to the side of the building and didn't get hurt.

"That was lucky!" Alma said. "See? Everything's fine. You don't have to worry about a bad fortune! I'm not a talented fortune-teller like you."

Alma was absolutely positively sure this was true. Everything was fine. She wasn't very good at magic or fortunes. She was just regular old Alma. And now she'd be able to go back to being shy, nervous Alma, and Del could go back to being brave, daring, and delightful Del, and all would be right at 86 ½ Twenty-Third Avenue.

Except.

Del was pointing at something.

She was pointing at her family's white car.

But it wasn't white anymore. The can of blue

paint had splattered all over the car. Big splashes of blue covered the whole thing.

"A blue car," Del said. "Just like your fortune said."

Closed Eyes

-Del-

As if it wasn't bad enough that Del's father's car was now blue, someone else was watching the whole scene.

Someone very scary.

The same black kitten from yesterday. It was dipping its paw into the blue paint, running away, then doing it again. It looked like it was trying to understand the paint, just like it had done with the water in the birdbath. It was quite the curious scientist. Maybe Del would have thought it was cute, once. But now it just seemed strange and scary and wrong. Why was this kitten everywhere all the time? Why wouldn't it leave them alone? And why didn't it act like the other stray cats in the neighborhood?

Little blue paw prints were taking over the sidewalk and street in front of Del's house, and they made Del even more scared. She ran inside and hid behind Abuelita's biggest, softest armchair. She was pretty sure a black cat couldn't find her back there. She didn't want that strange little kitten coming anywhere near her. It was dangerous! And bad! And who knew what would happen if she didn't hide from it! If Cassie could break her leg from seeing a black cat, Del would probably go through even worse because of her black cat fortune! It just wasn't safe to do anything at all.

Still, it wasn't very fun to hide behind a chair all day. Del called out for Alma.

"Are you okay?" Alma asked when she found her behind the chair.

"Right now I am," Del said. "As long as that cat doesn't find me, I'll be fine. But I'm bored."

"I've never seen a cat at the playground," Alma said. "Why don't we go over there?"

"I can't go back outside!" Del said. "Every time I go outside, that scary kitten finds me!"

"You've barely been outside," Alma said.

"Well, when I *was* outside, the kitten found me," Del said. She crossed her arms over her chest. She could be stubborn when she needed to be. And if she was going to avoid that black cat, she'd have to be very stubborn.

"Well, what do you want to do if we can't go outside?" Alma asked.

Del was willing to do anything to forget about the crystal ball and her bad fortune. She and Alma played eighteen rounds of Candyland with Evie, and it didn't help at all. Del taught Alma how to sing "Pon Pon Pon," the song Abuelita always sang to Del when she was little. That made Del happy for a little bit, but she quickly felt scared again. She tried drawing pictures and practicing cartwheels and visiting all her titis. She even tried cleaning her room! None of it helped.

Del had loved that crystal ball. She loved magic. And she loved Alma for giving her the special present. She didn't like being the fraidy-cat cousin.

"Maybe we can go outside for a little bit," Del said. "But I'm going to close my eyes, and if you see the cat or hear it or anything at all, we're going right back inside."

"Okay," Alma said. Del closed her eyes as tight as she could. Alma grabbed her hand and led her to the playground. Every few steps Del would ask if the kitten was there. It didn't matter how many times Alma told her everything was fine. Del was still scared.

She didn't get less scared at the playground. With her eyes closed, Del kept hearing noises that she was sure were that dangerous black kitten. Some scratching on the slide sounded like a kitten clawing at the plastic. Alma insisted that was just a little kid playing with a branch. Next, Del was sure she heard the kitten meowing. Alma told her that it was just a very squeaky swing.

When Del felt something soft brush against her ankles, she screamed. "It found me!"

Alma rushed to her side. The black kitten was nowhere to be found. Del's favorite dog, Oscar, was just trying to say hello.

Del bent down to let Oscar lick her hand.

But just when she decided to relax and enjoy her friend Oscar, the kitten appeared again. It ran right up to Oscar and batted his fluffy white tail with its tiny paw. A kitten that small should be scared of a dog, even a cute white fluffy one. But this kitten wasn't scared at all. Only curious. And determined. And Oscar didn't seem to mind. He wagged his tail in response, causing

the kitten to bat it even harder.

Evie watched, delighted.

Alma giggled and tried to find someone with a phone to take a photo.

But Del ran straight out of the playground and all the way back to her room. She dove

right under the covers.

That black kitten wouldn't be able to find her there.

. . . She hoped.

10

A Cursed Cousin

-Alma-

Alma wasn't sure how to help Del. She wasn't used to being the brave cousin. Or the in-charge cousin.

"What do we do?" Evie asked, and Alma didn't know how to answer.

"Do you think I'm cursed?" Alma asked her littlest cousin. "Do you think I can only tell bad fortunes?"

Evie thought about it. "Maybe," she said. She didn't seem very worried about it, though.

Maybe all along, *Evie* was the brave cousin. "We should ask Abuelita. She'll know."

Abuelita knew the answers to most things. She knew how much frosting was the perfect amount of frosting to put on a cupcake, and she knew where to find a cool costume, and she knew how to make a garden grow really fast, and how to make perfect rice and beans every time. And she knew all about magic.

Evie and Alma found Abuelita in the backyard garden when they got home. She was pulling weeds. Titi Clara was there too, helping. They both had large glasses of Abuelita's famous lavender lemonade and they were talking very quickly, half in Spanish, half in English. Alma could have sat all day and listened to the pretty way the two languages sounded together. But she didn't have all day. She had to help Del right now.

"Abuelita," Alma said, "do you think I'm cursed? Do you think all my fortunes are bad?"

Abuelita smiled. "I don't believe in curses," she said.

"But you believe in magic," Alma said.

"Those are very different things," Abuelita said.

"How?" Alma asked.

Abuelita gave her Abuelita shrug. One slow shrug. One very fast shrug. And a lift of her eyebrows. "You'll see," she said at last.

Alma wanted to believe Abuelita. And she almost did.

"Ouch!" Titi Clara yelped. Alma turned to face her. Titi Clara shook out her hand. "I got pricked by that rose's thorn!" she said. "I guess I'm not much of a gardener."

The rose was red. Just like Madame Alma had predicted it would be. And when Alma counted the number of red roses on the bush, there were exactly twelve.

A dozen red roses for Titi Clara.

Alma's heart sank. Another one of her Madame Alma fortunes gone bad.

Abuelita might not have believed in curses, but Alma was sure starting to.

The Very Scary Shadow

-Del-

That night, Del couldn't sleep. Every creak of the building made her nervous. She tossed and turned and tried to think of not-scary things like empanadas, and Oscar in the fancy black jacket and top hat he wore to Del's birthday party, and the silly songs Evie sometimes sang to make Del laugh.

But that kitten kept creeping into her thoughts. She imagined the scary kitten eating all their empanadas. The kitten in a tux,

sneaking up on Oscar. The kitten singing a scary song. Del just couldn't get away from thoughts of that kitten.

The kitten didn't act the way Del expected a kitten to act. That might have been what scared her most of all. She wanted to understand her fortune and the crystal ball and that little black kitten.

But she didn't understand any of it. And that made her want to hide away for as long as she could.

Del tried to close her eyes again. She shut them tight. She tried to order herself to sleep, but her body wouldn't listen. When she opened her eyes again, Del saw the scariest thing she'd ever seen. An enormous shadow of the kitten was on her wall. The kitten was now the size of a horse! It moved its legs and tail in a scary way. Del thought she might cry.

"Please go away!" she said to the kitten. But the shadow stayed. If anything, it grew bigger and closer.

"Leave me alone, kitten!" she said. But the kitten's shadow only stomped its scary paw.

Del hid under her covers, all the way at the bottom of the bed in a little ball. She would have to stay there until morning. Maybe she would have to stay there all week. Or all month! She didn't know when the kitten would finally go away and find another family to scare.

Meanwhile, the kitten didn't have any idea how scared she was making Del.

The kitten didn't know it was supposed to be bad luck.

The kitten didn't know it didn't act like a usual kitten. The kitten didn't know most kittens were scared of water and of dogs.

The kitten especially didn't know that its shadow looked so big and scary. The kitten was still just a very small kitten. Its shadow was large because of the position of Del's night-light.

And the kitten wasn't stomping its paw or

batting its tail around to be mean or scary or a monster.

The kitten had climbed into the tree outside Del's window and it had found a silver streamer from Del's birthday party.

The kitten loved that silver streamer. It batted the streamer, watched it move around, then

batted it again. It was even more fun than batting Oscar's tail! When the kitten accidentally pawed the streamer so hard that it fell to the ground, the kitten curled up in the crook of the tree and fell asleep. It dreamed of silver streamers and birdbaths and blue paint.

Del didn't sleep at all. And she didn't look outside her window to see how cute and small the kitten looked when it slept. She stayed at the bottom of her bed, underneath all her blankets, wishing she'd never ever seen that crystal ball or that little black kitten.

When Del got out of bed, she saw little blue paw prints all over the tree and the sidewalk in front of her building.

She felt her heart speed up. It felt extra big and extra loud. It made her ears ring and her mouth dry. It made her hands all sweaty even though they were also cold.

Del didn't understand why those paw prints

were still there or what the kitten had been doing or why. She didn't understand anything but how scared she was.

And now she was more scared than ever.

12

An Important Mission

-Alma-

There was one fortune from Madame Alma that still hadn't come true. She'd told Evie that she'd seen a mirror in the crystal ball. It hadn't happened yet, but Alma knew that if Evie got her hands on a mirror—any mirror—something terrible would happen.

So Alma did what she had to do. She needed to protect her family from her cursed fortunes.

But she needed Del to help her. She knocked and knocked on Del's door.

"I can't come out!" Del called out at last.

"There's still Evie's fortune," Alma said. "That hasn't come true yet!"

"It will," Del said. "And when it does, it will probably be terrible."

Del didn't sound like Del at all.

"I won't let it come true!" Alma called back.

"Be careful," Del said. She sounded tired. Fear was really exhausting, Alma knew.

Alma had a mission. She would make sure that Evie's fortune never came true. And if Evie's fortune didn't come true, then maybe Del would stop being so scared, and everything could go back to the way it was supposed to be.

Alma went into every single room in all of 86 ½ Twenty-Third Avenue. She was looking for all the mirrors. She started on the top floor, where her family lived. She covered all the bathroom mirrors with towels and carried all the smaller mirrors out to Abuelita's garden. She wasn't quite sure what she should do with them, but maybe Abuelita would be able to help. At least this way, Evie couldn't get hurt by her mirror fortune.

The second-highest floor belonged to Evie and her parents and Titi Rosa. Alma found a small handheld mirror in Titi Rosa's room and a pair of mirror earrings in Evie's mom's room. Alma tried to move Titi Rosa's full-length mirror, but it was too heavy to do on her own. She'd have to find some help.

Next, Alma went through Del's home. She found a few compacts from Del's mom and a pretty mirror that hung in Del's family's kitchen. Alma asked Del if she could look in her room for mirrors, and Del said no, but she opened the door a crack and handed Alma the mirror from her wall. It was the size of a book and had Del's name on it. It was one of Del's prized possessions.

Abuelita's home didn't have many mirrors, so Alma's work was almost done. The garden was full of mirrors now. Alma was very careful with each of them, lining them up against the fence, making sure they were all standing up so that no one would accidentally step on a mirror and hurt themselves.

There was just the one big mirror left. Titi Rosa's mirror. The one Evie loved. Alma couldn't ask Evie to help her remove it, of course—Evie needed to stay far away from mirrors. Alma called Felix Sanderson's house, but he was at soccer practice. Titi Clara's finger would probably hurt too much from the rose prick to help Alma carry the mirror, and Alma's parents would think she was being silly.

Alma needed her cousin. Her formerly brave, formerly up-for-anything cousin.

She needed Del.

13

A Dozen Cats

-Del-

Del had planned to stay in her room forever, but by about noon she was feeling pretty tired of hiding. Her room felt hot and stuffy. She'd left the book she was reading in Abuelita's living room. And she hadn't remembered to bring up any food to her room.

Plus, Del could hear all kinds of things happening on the street below. She heard her father laugh. She heard Titi Rosa singing. She heard Cassie and Anna and Evie drawing in chalk in front of the building, and she heard Oscar barking with excitement, like he did whenever he saw someone he wanted to play with.

If it weren't for that scary black cat, Del could be outside with her friends and family right now! She wished the cat would just go away, bother another building on another street. She didn't understand why the cat had to be hanging around 86 ½ Twenty-Third Avenue anyway.

By the time Alma knocked on her door again, Del was hungry and bored and hadn't heard a single meow or purr in hours. Maybe it was safe to go outside, she thought. Just for a moment. Or at least downstairs for some cremita.

"Del, I need your help," Alma said, knocking hard on her door. "Just for a minute. Just to protect Evie from the mirrors."

"Is the cat out and about?" Del asked.

"I haven't seen it all morning," Alma said.

"Yesterday you promised to protect me from it . . . ," Del started.

"I didn't expect it to come up to Oscar!" Alma said. "I thought cats were scared of dogs!"

"I don't understand that cat," Del said. "That's what's so scary about it."

"I guess," Alma said.

Del's stomach growled. "I can help for one minute. And maybe I can eat a little lunch. But then I'm coming right back up here forever," she said.

"That's fair," Alma said, opening Del's bedroom door.

The girls walked right upstairs to Titi Rosa's. There was the beautiful mirror. The last thing left to take down to the garden and get away from Evie. Evie was little. She needed to be protected. And even though Del was scared, she still took her responsibility as a big cousin very seriously.

Del and Alma were careful as they snuck the mirror out of Titi Rosa's home and down the stairs. They listened for Evie's little voice to

make sure she didn't catch them. Evie needed to stay as far away from the mirror as possible.

Alma opened the door to Abuelita's backyard garden, but before Del could put the mirror down somewhere safe, she gasped.

There in the garden, she saw dozens and dozens of black cats. Tall black cats. Skinny black

cats. Stumpy black cats. Black cats with tails that looked too long for their bodies. Black cats with smushy faces and black cats with especially long faces. Del had never seen so many cats at once. She had tried so hard to stay away from the little black kitten, and now she was in a garden of black cats.

Del screamed. That made Alma scream.

And with Del and Alma both screaming, something else happened. Those dozens of black cats all started to run at the same time. They ran. They leaped. And there was a crash!

The mirror Del and Alma were holding broke.

Del figured it must be one of the evil black cats.
Her bad fortune was finally beginning.

But when Del looked to try to see which black
cat had broken Titi Rosa's beautiful mirror, she
saw something she hadn't expected.

A dozen black cats lying down, meowing and
licking their paws.

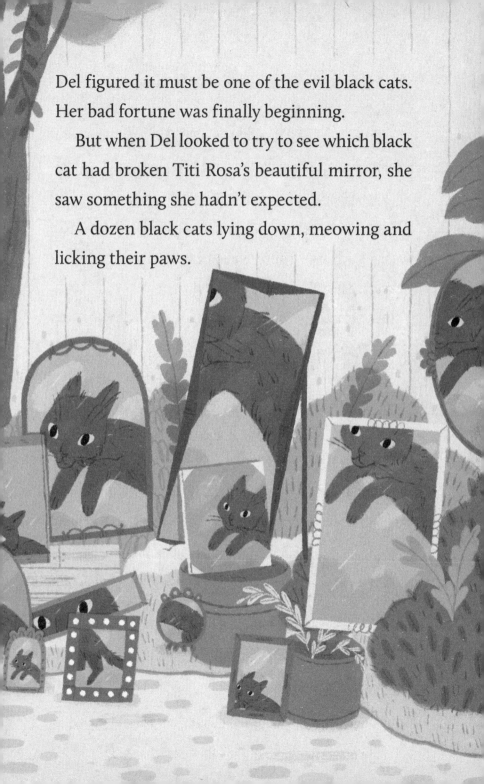

That was strange. That didn't make any sense at all.

"Why are all the cats hurt?" Del asked.

"There's only one cat, Del," Alma said.

"What do you mean?" Del asked. "Look around—there are— Oh." Del looked around. It did look like there were cats everywhere. But in fact, there were actually *mirrors* everywhere. There was only one cat being reflected in all the mirrors Alma had brought outside. The mirrors had been at all different angles, making the cats look like *they* were different shapes and sizes. But it was all the same single cat.

One little black kitten.

One hurt little black kitten.

14

Fraidycat

-Alma-

"What do we do?" Alma asked. She was panicked. She had never seen a cat get hurt before. And it was all her fault. She had told the terrible fortunes. She had bought the crystal ball. She had thought of the plan to bring all the mirrors outside.

Everything Alma had done had gone horribly wrong.

All this time Del had been worried about her bad fortune. But Alma was the one who couldn't do anything right, no matter how hard she tried!

"You should go upstairs," Alma said to Del. "You have to protect yourself from the kitten! Who knows what will happen!"

But Del didn't look so scared of the kitten anymore. In fact, Del was very carefully tiptoeing over to it. She was whispering something to it. She was petting its little head.

"This kitten needs our help," Del said. "Get some milk. And water. And a dishtowel. And Abuelita."

"But aren't you scared of the kitten?" Alma asked.

Alma and Del looked at the little kitten. It was shivering. It was curling itself into a ball. It looked scared. More scared than Alma had been at the party and more scared than Del had been since getting her fortune told.

"I think the kitten is the scared one now," Del said. She petted the kitten's head with one gentle finger. Alma ran inside to get Abuelita and water and milk and a towel. And when she returned with all those things, Del was holding the kitten in her lap.

She was singing it "Pon Pon Pon," the little song Abuelita used to sing her. She was telling it everything would be okay. She was showing it the bracelet on her wrist, and letting the kitten bat the sparkly charm back and forth.

"I thought you couldn't be anywhere near our little gato," Abuelita said when she saw them.

"It was hurt," Del said. "I know what I need when I'm hurt."

"I thought you thought the kitten was strange," Alma said. "I thought you didn't understand the fortune or the kitten."

Del shrugged. Del's shrug was a lot like an Abuelita shrug. A little mysterious. A little slow. A little magical.

"We're all a little strange sometimes, I guess," Del said.

"And the fortune?" Abuelita asked. She had a twinkle in her eye.

"Being scared of the fortunes only made things worse," Del said.

Alma nodded. She couldn't have agreed more. "I thought maybe if I could stop Evie's fortune from coming true, everything would be okay . . . ," Alma said.

"And that only caused trouble," Del finished.

"I guess we don't really understand fortunes," Alma said.

"Or crystal balls," Del said.

"Or kittens," Alma said.

"Or magic," Abuelita said.

"Especially magic," Alma said.

"But we don't have to understand everything," Del said.

"We don't?" Alma asked.

Del did an Abuelita shrug again. Abuelita did one too. "We all get scared sometimes," Del said. She held the kitten closer and wrapped the dishtowel around its hurt paw. She let it drink milk out of her hands. "And there will always be something or someone we don't really understand."

The kitten still looked scared. Del looked a little scared too. Alma supposed that was something they all had in common.

"Look at it," Alma said. "Just a little fraidycat, like me."

Del grinned. The kitten was purring. It would still have to go to the vet, but it was already feeling so much better, Alma was sure.

"What?" Alma asked. "Why are you smiling like that?"

"That's the perfect name for our kitten," Del said. "You're not the fraidycat anymore. Neither am I. The kitten is. We'll name it Fraidycat."

"I like that," Alma said. She was happy to not be the only fraidycat anymore. Everyone was a fraidycat sometimes, after all.

The Best Fortune-Teller Around

-Del-

The vet said Del had done a very good job taking care of Fraidycat. He also told them that Fraidy-cat was a girl cat and that she was under one year old and was very lucky indeed to have met Alma and Del. The vet sent Fraidycat home with some bandages and a little dropper of medicine and orders to bring her back in a week.

"Oh," Del said. "She's not ours."

"She's not?" the vet asked.

"She's not?" Abuelita asked with a glimmer in her eye.

"We can keep her?" Del asked. She raised her eyebrows. Her heart thumped. A tiny black kitten would be the best birthday present of all.

"I don't think we have much choice," Abuelita said. She nodded at Fraidycat, who was curled up and purring in Del's lap. Cats usually were scared of the vet, but Fraidycat didn't seem very afraid at all when Del was around.

Back home, Del and Alma gave Fraidycat a tour of 86 ½ Twenty-Third Avenue. Fraidycat was a little afraid of the stairs and Evie's talking baby doll and Titi Rosa's rocking chair.

But Fraidycat loved the long pink curtains in Alma's living room and the tassels on Abuelita's rug and the wind chimes hanging in Del's kitchen window.

What Fraidycat loved most of all, though, was the crystal ball. She found it in Del's closet and

curled herself around it. She pawed at its surface. She ran in circles around it, then nuzzled her nose against it, purring.

Alma and Del watched her play with the crystal ball.

"She's not afraid of that, I guess," Alma said.

"I guess not," Del said.

"What about you?" Alma asked. "Are you still afraid?"

"A little," Del said. "I'm still scared my bad fortune will come true."

"But your fortune did come true," Alma said. "And it wasn't bad at all."

"It did?" Del asked. She'd been so busy worrying about something horrible happening, she hadn't thought about what had *actually* happened. A black cat had come into her life, just like Madame Alma had predicted. "Oh!" Del said. "Oh my gosh! You're right! I got a black cat, just like you predicted!" Del's eyes were wide. She felt the way she always felt when magic was around—excited and in awe and ready for anything.

Well, almost anything.

"I guess not all my fortunes are cursed after all," Alma said. "But still, I don't think I'll be turning into Madame Alma again anytime soon."

"I don't think I want to be Madame Del again either," Del said.

"There's really only one person who wants to use that crystal ball," Alma said. "One cat, that is."

Fraidycat purred and waved her tail. Her tiny tongue licked the crystal ball's surface.

"Madame Fraidycat," Del said.

Fraidycat purred in agreement.

Alma and Del leaned in close to the ball. They wondered if Madame Fraidycat could see anything inside. They wondered if they could see what she saw. What might their future hold? What kinds of adventures were ahead for them?

And there, reflected in the crystal ball's crystal surface, were Alma and Del and their itty-bitty Fraidycat, all smiling and hopeful and not so scared after all.

A very happy fortune indeed.

Acknowledgments

I love spending time in the world of these books, and I'm so thrilled to keep hanging out on Twenty-Third Avenue.

Many thanks to my agent, Victoria Marini, for helping me find the imperfect in the beautiful.

Such a big thank-you to my editor, Mabel Hsu, for taking ideas and making them into magic. Your vision and clarity have proven to be so necessary and inspiring for me.

Thank you, Katherine Tegen, for your ongoing enthusiasm and support.

A very special thank-you to incredible illustrator Luisa Uribe. I see myself and my friends and family in your illustrations, and it brings me so much joy.

Thank you to designer David L. DeWitt for

helping make this book truly beautiful and love filled.

Thank you so much to Alexandra Hernandez. I love sharing stories with you.

Thank you to the wonderful team at Katherine Tegen Books who give so much of themselves to the work of bringing books into the world, and who have treated my books with incredible care: Tanu Srivastava, Amy Ryan, Alexandra Rakaczki, Maya Myers, Allison C. Brown, Emma Meyer, Sam Benson, and Robert Imfeld.

And a big thank-you to the readers who keep showing up for my books. You make me brave.

Alma and Del's magical mishaps
and fun continue in:

Read on for a sneak peek!

Stripes and Flowers and Polka Dots and Plaid

-Alma-

When Cassie came into the Curious Cousins Secondhand Shoppe, Alma could tell she knew exactly what she wanted.

"That," Cassie said. She pointed her finger at the purse that had been hanging in the window all month. It was a patchwork bag, made from at least thirty different fabrics. It was yellow and silver and blue and purple. It had stripes and florals and polka dots and plaids. Parts of it sparkled. Parts of it shined.

It was beautiful. It was special. It was strange. And it was supposed to be Alma's.

"Oh," Alma said sadly. "Are you sure?"

"Totally sure!" Cassie replied. "I've been saving up for the entire school year to buy something special. And this is it. This is my something special."

Alma nodded. Cassie had talked for months about coming into the store to buy her something special. And Alma had been excited to see what she would pick! But she never imagined Cassie would pick the perfect patchwork purse. Alma wasn't sure if she believed in magic, but that purse looked magical. It looked like maybe, *maybe*, it might be the kind of magic Alma could finally understand.

And Alma didn't know how to say that to Cassie.

"Great pick!" Alma's cousin and best friend, Del, said. "That purse is *really* special."

Alma's littlest cousin, Evie, ran to get the

ladder so she could be the one to climb up to get the purse. Their family cat, Fraidycat, bounded behind her. Fraidycat was always curious, and Evie was always doing something that made her extra-curious. Maybe Evie was Fraidycat's something special.

Alma had been thinking the purse was *her* something special. She had been the first person to see the purse. She'd been helping Abuelita go through bags of donations and the purse had been at the very bottom of one. At first, Alma thought it was weird. Maybe even ugly. But the more the purse hung in the window, the more beautiful it became.

Alma loved having the purse in the window. It reminded her that even though she didn't believe in magic the way Del did or the way Abuelita did—which was a whole lot—she believed things were not always what they seemed. She believed that something ordinary could become something special. And she believed that maybe, someday she'd be the kind of person who could use a magical-looking purse like that.

Alma was thinking all that, but it sounded too silly to say out loud.

"It's very expensive," Alma said to Cassie instead of all the other much truer things she wanted to say.

"I looked at the price tag," Cassie said. "It's going to be perfect for all the end of the school year stuff—the parade and the picnic and everything else. I can put my sunglasses in it. And books. And a hat."

Evie came back with the ladder. She was grunting and gasping, pulling the ladder through the store all by herself. Fraidycat swung her tail around, as if she was helping, too. "I'll get the purse for you!" Evie said excitedly. Fraidycat meowed in agreement.

"We should ask Abuelita if the purse is really for sale," Alma said. She knew she sounded silly. The purse was hanging in the window! Of course it was for sale!

It was too late, anyway. Evie was scrambling up the ladder and Cassie was counting out her money and Del was heading to the back to get Abuelita to ring it up.

Alma kept trying to think of a way to explain why she wanted that purse to stay put. She wanted to be able to say loving that purse made her feel more like the rest of her family at 86 ½ Twenty-Third Avenue. She wanted to tell them all how special she felt when she was the one who found it. And how when it glittered a certain way, it made her think maybe Abuelita was right, that magic was everywhere.

"¡Qué maravilloso!" Abuelita said when she saw the purse on Cassie's shoulder. And Abuelita

was right, the purse was truly marvelous. It was just what Abuelita had said when Alma had first shown it to her. "It really suits you."

Alma thought she might cry.

She wanted Abuelita to tell her that the purse suited *her*. She wanted someone to think *she* should have a sparkly and plaid and flowery and stripy and polka-dotted purse.

Alma wiped away a tear. She swallowed hard. She tried one more time to think of the right words to explain to everyone why Cassie shouldn't have that purse.

But no one even noticed.

Cassie was too happy looking at her brand-new purse. Del and Abuelita and Evie were too busy admiring how the purse looked on Cassie.

As usual, Alma was quiet.

She watched as Cassie skipped out of the Curious Cousins Secondhand Shoppe.

"I thought it was supposed to be mine," Alma said. But no one heard.

6